PERSONAL TRAINER

BLACK AND BEAUTIFUL EROTICA 1.
NICOLAS BLANC

For information on hot new releases and a free erotica ebook subscribe to

CHAPTER 1. JAY

Emily Anderson, twenty-eight, curly-haired and curvy, had been dreading meeting the personal trainer. Emily preferred the world of books to the physical world and liked exercising her mind and not her body. Ever since being hit in the ear playing softball at school she was convinced that bad things happen outside.

Mia, Emily's best friend had guilted her into having a session with Mia's personal trainer. Emily had agreed to it just to get Mia off her back but now the fateful day had arrived Emily was filled with a sense of dread.

Jay, the personal trainer recognized Emily straight away in the park and Mia had described Emily very well. Emily wore her favorite tracksuit, mismatched tracksuit pants and jacket, both of which she had purchased over ten years ago. Fashions had come and gone so much that her mismatched old school style had come back into fashion. Emily wore some flat-soled sneakers, which she found buried at the bottom of her wardrobe. Her freckled face was framed with a peaked New York Yankees hat, barely containing her frizzy red hair.

"Emily?" Jay said.

"Hi," Emily said shaking Jay's hand.

"I thought we would start with something fairly light today. Mia told me you haven't been doing much exercise."

"Yeah, I don't do any apart from walking to the subway," Emily said slightly raising her shoulders.

"Well we're going to have to change that," Jay said with a disapproving look.

"OK," said Emily trying to think of excuses to get out of the fitness session.

"First, let's do a slow jog around the lake," Jay said, "Follow me."

I'll show him, thought Emily and took off fast like a foal that was running for the first time, fast but slightly awkward. Emily sprinted past Jay but it was not long until she was hunched over and gasping for breath.

"Are you a smoker?" Jay asked.

"No," Emily said looking up, sweaty and red-faced.

"I think we should walk for a bit," said Jay.

They walked around the lake silently until Emily got her breath back.

"Feel better?" Jay asked.

Emily nodded.

"OK," said Jay, "Let's do some stretches."

They found a shady area of grass.

"First let's stretch out the back. Reach up high like this and then touch your toes," Jay demonstrated raising his hands above his head, Emily could not help but notice Jay's shirt rise up revealing a glimpse of his taut lower abdomen before he bent down to touch his toes.

Emily found she could replicate the stretch up but could not reach down anywhere near her toes.

Emily tried to avoid Jay's disapproving look as she stood up again, instead choosing to look over Jay's shoulder, causing Jay to look behind himself to see what Emily was looking at. There was a hotdog stand there. Jay just shook his head slightly.

"I wasn't thinking of food," Emily said.

Jay just slightly raised his eyebrows and said, "We got some work to do."

CHAPTER 2. MIA

Emily's second session with Jay was at the local 24-hour gym.

"OK Emily, watch me," Jay said before seating himself in a lat pulldown, his muscles bulging each time he pulled down upon the bar.

Jay then reduced the weight down by half.

"OK, your turn. Keep the movement nice and smooth," he said.

Emily tried to slowly pull down upon the bar of the machine but found she could not lift the weight at all.

"Hold on I'll make an adjustment," said Jay, reducing the weight rating again by half, "OK, try that."

That's better, thought Emily. She could actually pull down upon the bar and lift the weight.

Emily gave Jay a goofy smile. He smiled quickly and then said, "Very good but keep it nice and slow and smooth. The smoother the movement the less chance of strain."

"Hey guys," Mia said approaching them, "How's it going?"

"Fine, I guess," said Emily," What are you doing here?"

"I'm a member here," said Mia, "Jay introduced me to this gym and it's just around the corner from my apartment."

"OK Emily, let's try pulling down on the bar again," Jay said.

Emily pulled the bar down with ease.

"Not bad. I can see Jay is whipping you into shape," said Mia, "Pretty soon you'll be able to keep up with me and we can go jogging."

Mia went onto the machine next to Emily and was soon pulling a much heavier weight than Emily.

"OK, I'm ready for a heavier weight," said Emily.

Mia followed Emily and Jay right around all the equipment in the gym, the competition forcing Emily to push herself to her limits.

"OK, that's enough," Jay said, "I don't want you to be hurting too much tomorrow."

"I'll stop when Mia stops," Emily said under her breath.

"Mia's been training for years. You need to slowly build up to long exercise routines. Now hit the showers, please," said Jay with a wry smile on his face.

Emily reluctantly finished her exercise and walked off to the changing rooms.

"Hey, thanks for referring Emily to me," Jay said as Mia lifted a barbell with weights that seemed far too heavy for her.

"My pleasure," Mia said, "Before long she'll be a new woman."

As Mia's arms shook with the weight of the barbell Jay moved the back of his hand along Mia's side, brushing his hand back and forward against the side of her nipple, scanning her face for a reaction.

Jay leaned down low so that Mia could feel his breath upon her face.

"You know I love it when I see you sweat," Jay whispered.

Mia placed the barbell down upon its rest then looked into Jay's eyes which were as steely as a panther. Jay then leaned in and kissed Mia gently on the lips.

"What if Emily comes back?" Mia said.

Jay kissed her again, firmer and more urgently this time, first on the lips then down along her neck. Mia reacher her hand out behind Jay's head and stretched her fingers through his hair, massaging the back of his head as he kissed her.

Jay pulled the tops of Mia's gym shirt down over her shoulders and kissed each shoulder in turn as Mia closed her eyes. Jay then pressed his lips onto Mia's forehead, breathing in her musky scent, a mixture of sweat and perfume.

"You smell good," Jay said looking Mia in the eyes.

"So do you," Mia said, moving her hand over Jay's muscular chest, her hand gently tracing each bump and curve on his lower abdomen then chest.

"Have you had sex with her yet?" Mia asked.

Jay stood up and looked offended, "I don't have sex with all my clients. I'm a personal trainer, not a male gigolo."

"I'm sorry," Mia said

"And anyway my sex life is private. I'm sure you wouldn't like me talking about you with other people," Jay said. The mood had changed.

"I'm sorry Jay," Mia said, "Please forgive me."

"That's OK. Look I should be having a shower and getting changed anyway. It's late," Jay said.

Mia sighed as she watched Jay head off to the changerooms. *Damn, he is a handsome man*, she thought.

CHAPTER 3. INVITATION

Mia had known Emily since high school. Mia had always been the one popular with the boys. Emily had been the bookworm, pretty with pale freckled skin and beautiful green eyes but too shy to flirt with the boys.

Mia was the polar opposite of Emily – a sleek Puerto Rican who boys would stop to watch when she walked into the room just in love with the way she walked. Mia was also super organized; always at least two or three steps ahead of the competition while Emily was one of those people who had a genius level of intelligence but was very disorganized and found basic life skills a challenge, including developing and managing relationships.

Even at college, Emily had been on very few dates. When she did go out it tended to be going out with Mia, her current boyfriend, and his friend. The chances of 'the friend' having common interests with Emily were always slim. Mia liked the athletic boys, slim and muscular. They tended to have similar friends who were heavily into sports but not into books and movies like Emily who spent much of the time smiling shyly while pretending to know what the others were talking about when they discussed basketball, baseball or football.

Mia even suspected that Emily was still a virgin. *She deserved more* thought, Mia, looking out her apartment window at the city lights sparkling below. Emily just needed to develop some self-confidence, she thought.

Jay was the best lover Mia had ever had and still thought about him late at night in her bed. Sometimes she closed her eyes and pictured Jay above her instead of Arnold her current boyfriend when they made love. Mia knew though that Jay would never settle down with any one woman. It was obvious he loved women but she suspected that someone he loved had broken his heart and would not be able to wholly trust a woman again.

The next morning Mia and Emily met for coffee at the local Starbucks.

"So how are things working out with Jay?" asked Mia, licking the cappuccino froth from her top lip.

"I am feeling fitter," Emily said with a smile, "and I've dropped a dress size."

"Well done," said Mia raising her coffee and toasting Emily.

"I'm not getting puffed going upstairs any longer," Emily said with a giggle.

"Awesome. We'll have to go shopping together. I know just the place," said Mia.

"I've found a place online as well. They have some nice designs," said Emily playing with her phone and then bringing up a clothing website.

Mia looked at the website but had to silently suppress a yawn when examining what was on offer.

"Hey Mia, excuse me a moment. I'll be back in a sec," Emily said disappearing off to the bathroom.

Mia smiled to herself and thought for a second. *This is too delicious*, she said to herself as she went to Emily's contacts.

"There we go – Jay," she said quietly, clicking on the message icon to send him a text – "Thinking about you. F."

"This is too naughty," Mia said smiling. Her finger hovered over the delete icon but then instead of delete she pressed send.

Mia watched the screen of Emily's iPhone, holding her breath.

A smiley face appeared in response to the message from Jay. "What a flirt," Mia said and noticed Emily approaching the table, quickly deleting both texts and bringing back the clothing website.

"You like?" Emily said.

"Yes, I do but I think you need something a little less librarian and a little more up for it sex queen," Mia said.

Emily laughed, "You're outrageous."

CHAPTER 4. AWAKENING

Emily had an appointment with Jay that afternoon. They met at Central Park.

Emily noticed that Jay was more friendly than normal, smiling as he gave Emily the instructions for her afternoon exercises. The smiles and positive feedback made Emily work harder at the exercises.

"Emily," Jay said at the end of the workout, standing closer to Emily than normal, "You have done really well today."

Emily smiled, "Well I have a good teacher."

Jay brushed a stray hand away from Emily's freckled face.

"You are making good progress," Jay said absentmindedly.

Jay was so close and Emily's eyes focused on his smooth dark skin and his lips.

Emily's hand moved up and brushed it across Jay's cheek. His skin was so smooth and soft.

Jay looked into Emily's eyes. Emily moved her hand behind Jay's head and pulled him towards her lips, stroking the back of his head as she breathed him into her, tilting her head back slightly as they kissed. Emily forgot they were in the park as everyone else and everything else just faded into the background.

Jay's hand clasped the small of Emily's back and he pulled her hips towards his. Emily looked around quickly and moved her eyes and head to indicate to move behind the nearby bushes.

Emily grasped Jay's hand as they moved to the more secluded area of the park. Jay peeled off his top without saying a word, his muscles rippling across his chest and stomach.

Emily also peeled off her top then walked towards Jay and jumped up into his arms, curling her legs around him. They kissed for what seemed to Emily to be an eternity, a fire burning from within her, pulsing along her veins. She could feel the fire within Jay as well, a powerful force pressing against her under his sports shorts.

Jay pressed up towards Emily, firm between her legs, rocking back and forth like he was in an altered state, intoxicated by her. Emily moved her hand around the bulge in his shorts, moving her hand back and forth rhythmically until Jay's erection peaked over the top of his shorts. Emily gasped and was transfixed at the size of Jay and the beauty of his erection.

Emily peeled Jay's shorts down his legs like she was peeling an exotic fruit, the cheeks of her face glanced across Jay's throbbing erection.

"Oh, Emily. That felt so good," Jay almost pleaded.

Emily checked to see if any passersby could observe them then bent down and delicately kissed along Jay's powerful shaft. Jay threw his head back, his hands running through Emily's curly hair, massaging her scalp.

Emily experimented by putting the small O of her mouth around the tip of Jay's erection. Just the slightest touch of her lips against the tip of Jay's penis made it grow further.

Emily checked again for passersby and then dropped to her knees and stroked Jay's shaft with her hand while nibbling the tip of his penis with her mouth and licking along the shaft. Emily looked up at Jay's face which was contorted with pleasure and was quite flattered that she had produced so much pleasure in Jay, her only education about what men liked gleaned from DH Lawrence and Anais Nin. This was her first man and he was magnificent, she thought.

Emily moved her mouth over the top of Jay's penis again. He was so hard. Emily moved her mouth as far down along Jay's shaft as she could, feeling him swell within her. She felt intoxicated by his desire for her and her own desire for Jay. It was like years of pent up sexual frustration were finally being released. Emily just did not care that they were in Central Park. She felt like this was the pinnacle of her life and no one would stop her now.

Jay moved very gently forward and back as Emily sucked him, his fingers stroking the back of her head, timing a slight hip thrust with when he would bring Emily's head forward. Emily felt her shorts were dripping as she bobbed her head up and down.

"Emily, this is too much. Slow down a little or I will cum," Jay said savoring every movement by Emily.

Emily looked up at Jay whose eyes were closed, lost in the moment. Jay then looked down at Emily and smiled, "Oh baby. I'm so close to the edge."

Emily looked around again. She could see a couple walking in the distance but there was no one who could see them. Emily pulled off her sports shirt and bra and pulled Jay close to her. Jay was warm and smooth and smelt like sandalwood. He grasped the back of her head and kissed Emily over and over while his erection pressed against her stomach.

Emily then wriggled out of her gym shorts and panties. Every sense in her body was focused on Jay as she slung one leg around him and lent up against a tree. Jay placed his hands on Emily's buttocks and smiled as he pulled Emily's body into his, Emily surprised at how easily he entered her. *Your first time was not meant to be this much fun*, she thought.

Emily looked into Jay's eyes as he pulsed within her. Jay thrust forcefully, Emily's back rubbing up against the bark of the tree. Jay moved his right hand from Emily's buttock and started to stroke between her legs as he continued to thrust into her, circling her clit with his thumb. He then lifted the hand to caress Emily's face then kissed her deeply as the intensity of his thrusting increased. The kiss stifled an involuntary moan from Emily as she felt the pressure released from between her legs, through her clit and tingle along her back and throughout her body.

CHAPTER 5. FACETIME

The next morning Emily lay on her bed smiling and thinking of Jay, thinking about how long until she had her next personal training session.

Emily's hand snaked down and lifted her nightdress and caressed the tops of her thighs as she thought about Jay's muscular body, powerful, dark and beautiful.

Emily's iPhone vibrated with a new message on the bedside table. Continuing to stroke herself she picked up the telephone and checked the message. It was from Jay.

"Loved spending time with you yesterday. J. x," it read.

He's on his phone, thought Emily, scrolling through her contacts to find Jay, personal trainer and pressing dial for a Facetime call.

"Hi Jay," Emily said breathlessly, still lying in her bed.

"Oh hi," Jay said, looking slightly sheepish, bright neon lights above his head.

"I've been thinking of you," Emily said, slipping a finger between her legs and massaging her nub.

"Ah ha," Jay said, looking around him.

"Your cock is amazing," Emily said.

Jay giggled and looked embarrassed.

"I can't wait until you are inside me again," Emily said, slightly panting as she continued to stroke herself.

"Are you doing what I think you're doing?" Jay whispered down the line.

"A lady never tells," Emily said coquettishly but the red flush on her cheeks gave the game away.

"You are too much," Jay said smiling.

"When are you coming over to see me?"

"It depends," Jay whispered into the telephone, the lights moved over his head.

"Depends on what?" Emily said.

"If you are ready for another workout," Jay said, a 'Sale' sign passing over his head.

"Are you in the supermarket?" Emily said, herself now giggling.

"Ah ha," Jay said smiling.

"I love working out," Emily said.

"OK, I'll be there in 10 minutes."

"I'll be ready. I'll do some warm-ups," Emily said, slipping her finger deeper into the wetness within her.

Emily then had a shower, continuing to caress herself, directing the shower spray between her legs to stimulate her clit, imagining Jay holding her again.

Emily then dried and combed her hair, put on a deep red lipstick and mascara, perfumed herself and sat in the sofa of her living room naked, stroking between her legs until she was wet and ready for Jay.

Just the sound of the knock on the door almost made Emily cum.

Jay sat up on the couch and spread her legs.

"Come on in, it's open," Emily said, a slight nervousness in her voice.

Jay entered the room.

"Wow," he said, quickly closing the door to Emily's apartment before any nosy neighbors could peek inside.

"Hi Jay," Emily said, trying very hard to resist the urge to close her legs and cover-up.

"You look amazing," Jay said, his eyes devouring every detail of Emily.

"Why thank you, Mr Jay," Emily said in a voice she had not heard herself use before.

Jay dropped his shopping by the door and came and hugged Emily's naked body to his then leaned down and took Emily's mouth in his. Jay slipped his hands under Emily's bottom and lifted her up and she hugged Jay like a koala.

"You are one sexy little lady," Jay whispered in Emily's ear then kissed Emily soft but urgent, "There's something about you that is amazing."

"I'm ready for my personal training," Emily whispered into Jay's ear, her heartbeat quickening.

Jay held Emily with one hand as he used his other hand to yank down his shorts and underwear.

"OK, now I want you to grip my cock firmly between your legs," Jay said, "And squeeze."

Jay then lowered Emily onto his erection. Emily found the sensation incredible, a shiver going down her spine.

"I've been thinking of you constantly since yesterday," Jay said.

"Me too," said Emily, slightly breathless as Jay kissed along her neck, lighting little fires, while her fingers gripped Jay's muscular shoulders.

The muscles in Jay's arms rippled against Emily as he lifted her up and down upon his rock hard cock.

"Jay before you cum, let's try something," said Emily.

"Oh, baby. Just a few more seconds," said Jay.

Emily tapped on Jay's shoulder, "Jay, listen. There's something I've always wanted to try."

Jay lowered Emily to the ground freeing his swollen penis which looked almost painfully erect.

"What is it, baby?" Jay said.

"I fantasize about being dominated," Emily said.

"You are really full of surprises," Jay said.

"Have you tried it before?" Emily asked.

"No. An old girlfriend did drag me along to *50 Shades of Grey* and we did experiment a little after that."

"I don't know why. Since I was a teenager I always found domination my go to sexual fantasy," Emily said.

"Do you ever keep any secrets?" Jay asked.

"I'm usually very shy. I don't know what's come over me."

"OK well give me five star jumps," Jay said half-jokingly but Emily immediately snapped into action and was jumping enthusiastically in the air, her breasts bouncing wildly up and down.

"Ah, now face the window, legs apart and bend down and touch your toes. Do it five times," said Jay.

Emily faced the window, spread her legs slightly and bent down to touch her toes, giving Jay a clear view of her vulva each time she bent down.

Jay had to admit that there was something kind of erotic about this and he wondered if he may cum just from watching Emily in such a wanton display.

On the last of the five bends, Jay said, "And hold."

He then stood close to Emily and examined her pale freckled skin and the pinkness of her vagina. He then leaned in and flicked his tongue onto her clit from behind.

"Oh," said Emily.

"Stay there," said Jay and then smacked her pale buttocks with his hand, leaving a bright pink mark.

"Ouch," said Emily.

Jay was worried. Had he gone too far?

"I'm sorry Emily. I didn't mean to hurt you," Jay said his arm around her.

"I loved it," said Emily looking around at him with a cheeky grin, "More please."

"More please, what?" Jay had a slight snigger in his voice.

"More please, sir," Emily said proudly.

Jay then slapped Emily on the buttocks again making a loud slap. He wondered for a moment what the neighbors may be thinking.

Jay then brought two slaps down on Emily's buttocks in quick succession. Emily's head hung low, her curly red hair falling over her face. She then reached around and parted her sex with two fingers and said, "Take me."

Jay put his finger to his lip and studied Emily. She was so wet and waiting for him. The fact that she was so aroused was very arousing for him.

Jay slipped a finger between Emily's legs and gently her inner thighs and gradually moved in and rubbed either side of her clit until he could hear her sigh. He then reached between her legs and grabbed between them, making her arch her back and stand on tippy toes.

"What would you like me to do?" Jay whispered in Emily's ear.

"Please take me, sir. I'm all yours," Emily said looking Jay intensely in the eyes.

Jay removed his hand and edged his penis up between her legs, rocking gently between them at first, and then edging in bit by bit with each thrust, grabbing Emily's red buttocks for leverage.

Emily was so wet and inviting, thrusting her bottom back into him until she had taken all of him between her legs. Emily sighed at the delicious fullness between her legs, the manly smell of Jay, his ardent thrusting, his sighs and finally the warm rush of his fluid.

CHAPTER 6. LEED

Even though they had become lovers Jay still provided personal training sessions to Emily who enthusiastically used the running machines and weights at the gym. The daily exercise sessions were followed by nights of passion. Emily lost weight, built up core strength and dropped dress sizes.

While exercising Emily felt Jay's intense stare upon her and she loved it. She took to wearing tight exercise pants and bras which showed off her new physique. Jay took personal pride in Emily's fitness and felt pride when he noticed the other guys in the gym checking out his girlfriend – just as long as they did not try any moves on her.

One night it was late and Emily and Jay were the last people left in the gym.

"Come here," said Jay, giving Emily a 'come hither' sign with his hand.

Emily left the exercise bike and walked towards Jay who was sitting on a weight bench after having lifted weights. Emily leaned down and kissed Jay who whispered, "Take off your shirt and wrap it around your eyes to make a blindfold."

Emily looked around, "Jay, what if someone comes in?"

"Who's going to come into the gym at this time of night?" Jay asked, "Now, are you going to be a good kitten and do what I say or will you have to be punished?"

Either option sounded quite enticing to Emily who was already starting to feel aroused.

Emily looked around again and then gingerly pulled off her shirt and tied it around her head.

"Very good, kitten," Jay said, "Now slip out of your bra, shorts, and panties and put your panties in your mouth."

Emily quickly followed Jay's instructions and soon stood pale, naked, blindfolded, gagged and fragile in the vastness of the gym.

"Now on the floor," Jay said and Emily moved from the bench to the floor.

"Get down on all fours," Jay commanded. He was getting the swing of this, as was the rather large swelling at the front of his shorts.

"Arch your back," Jay said, "OK, up, now down."

"OK, put your head down, low to the ground and your bottom up high."

Emily started to worry about someone coming into the gym.

"What if..." Emily mumbled through the panties.

"Did I say you could talk?" Jay said, spanking Emily's buttocks with his hand, leaving a red hand mark, and Emily's milky white skin blushed crimson.

Jay pulled up a chair and sat admiring Emily.

Jay studied every curve and crevice of Emily as if she was a foreign landscape. She wanted to transcend the everyday into something wild, powerful and dramatic.

Jay traced his finger down the nape of Emily's neck, along her spine and between her legs, stopping to play with her until his fingers became damp and her clitoris stood proud. Jay bent down and massaged it with his tongue flicking back and forth.

Emily moaned.

"Did I tell you that you could make a noise?" Jay chastised her.

Emily bit her lip.

Jay gently rubbed either side of Emily's clitoris with his fingers then returned to licking it and then gently sucking upon it until it was a hard little nub. While sucking, Jay reached around with his hands and massaged Emily's breasts and held her nipples and gently pulled them until they were also standing proud and hard.

Jay then stood up and walked around Emily.

Emily felt something cold around her neck which clicked together at the back.

"What's that?" Emily tried to say through the panties in her mouth.

"You thought I forgot your birthday but I didn't. It's a pearl necklace but no peeking for now," Jay said, his breath heavy, his hand stroking along Emily's bare leg.

"OK. Let's go for a walk," Jay said.

Emily opened her eyes and Jay held a long pearl rope which led to a pearl necklace around her neck.

Jay pulled on the rope and Emily crawled on the gym floor as Jay led her in a circle, enjoying the sway of her bottom and breasts as she moved.

Jay then led Emily to the men's change room and removed the pearl necklace from around her neck.

"Now open your legs towards the door," Jay said, "Wider please."

Emily spread her legs as far apart as she could.

"Good girl," Jay said, "Now open the lips with your fingers."

Emily used two fingers to hold her lips apart so Jay could see her pink inner core.

"Very good. Now use one hand to play with your breasts and your other one to play with your clit. That's it. You need to be good and wet for what I have in mind."

Jay watched Emily writhing on the men's change room floor, stroking her breasts and stroking between her legs, studying what gave her pleasure. He felt so powerful to have such a beautiful woman dedicated to him so thoroughly.

"I'll be back. Don't stop," Jay said going to the drink's machine and getting a coke and then going back to the change room where Emily was still stroking herself with her eyes closed and intensity in her face.

"Don't stop but don't cum," Jay said sitting down and sipping the coke while admiring Emily.

"Oh," Emily sighed on the brink of orgasm.

"Stop!" Jay commanded in a way that gave Emily a shock, "Now stand up, hands behind your head."

Jay felt between Emily's legs and rubbed his fingers together, "Very good."

Jay then picked up the pearl necklace and rope and hooked one end of it onto a hook on one side of the change room and hooked the other end on a hook on the other side of the change room.

"Now stand either side of the pearls, still with your arms above your head and walk from the middle to the end of the pearls."

Emily lifted her leg over the middle of the pearl rope so that it brushed against her leg.

"Move forward," Jay said.

Emily stepped forward and the pearls rubbed against her thigh.

"And again," Jay said.

Emily stepped forward and the pearls glanced against her inner thigh.

"And again," Jay said.

This time the pearls just touched the outer lips of Emily's sex, smooth and cold.

"And again," Jay said.

The pearls were now deeply between Emily's legs. Jay held the pearls on either side of Emily and moved them back and forth.

"And again," Jay said.

Emily now had to stand on her toes; the pearls were tightly between her legs, penetrating deeply between her lips.

Jay stroked Emily's breasts and then tweaked her nipples before kissing along her neck.

"One more step and you are there," Jay said.

Emily stood forward; she was now standing high on her toes.

Jay tickled either side of Emily's stomach causing a look of panic in her face.

"OK now move back to the middle," Jay said

Jay then lowered the pearl rope.

"You did well Emily. Good workout. You can now hit the showers," Jay said with a smile, pointing to the men's showers.

Emily removed her panties from her mouth and padded towards the men's shower cubicles.

Jay followed her into the small cubicle and kissed Emily, his powerful arms encircling her. He turned on the water and steamy hot water fell upon them as Jay thrust up into Emily who was so wet that she took his massive erection much more easily than previously. Slowly Jay thrust into Emily, efficiently but sensuously as her back pressed against the tiles of the shower, her leg wrapped around Jay's muscular lower torso. As Jay penetrated her deeper and deeper, he kissed and pecked at her neck, leaving a trail of love bites along it.

Jay watched Emily as she walked from the shower, drops of water falling from her soft curves, grabbed a fluffy white towel and turned and smiled and blew Jay a kiss.

Damn she was fine, thought Jay. *Watch it, man*, he told himself.

CHAPTER 7. BITES

Emily met Mia for coffee at the local Starbucks the following morning.

"Emily, you look amazing," said Mia, stretching out her hands as she had just been presented with a gift.

"Thanks, Mia. I love your handbag. Where did you get it?" Emily replied.

"I've had it for ages. Got it in the Macy's sales a couple of years ago," Mia said.

Emily's whole body ached and she felt a little unsteady like she had just stepped out of a dream.

They sat opposite each other at a table by the window. The rich smell of the coffee cleared Emily's head.

"Emily, now tell me – how *are* you?" Mia said.

"Everything's going really well," Emily said.

"I can see Jay is working wonders with you," Mia said looking Emily up and down.

"He is very talented," said Emily, "...as a personal trainer."

"I have to be honest. I almost did not recognize you when I first saw you. You have lost so much weight," Mia said. Emily noticed Mia's eyes glancing at her neck.

"Jay has a pretty tough training regime," Emily said.

"He sure does," Mia said, "He's very in demand."

Emily thought about this comment. *Exactly how many women Jay is sleeping with*, she wondered.

"My muscles are really aching at the moment I have to confess," Emily said.

"Listen I have some ointment at home that is fantastic for muscle aches. It's a secret recipe prepared by my Chinese herbalist," Mia said.

"Sounds good," said Emily.

"We can pop into my apartment after we finish here and I'll give you some," said Mia.

"Sure," said Emily.

Mia's apartment was the second from the top and had a bird's eye view of Central Park. It was already furnished when she bought it and she had held onto the furniture. In the lounge room, there were brown Chesterfield lounge chairs and a sofa. Leafy palms sat in ornate sandstone pots. It looked like an old school gentleman's club from the movies. Emily always half expected a white-suited waiter to come around the corner holding drinks on a silver platter.

"So where are you sore?" asked Mia, coming out to the balcony where Emily was admiring the view.

"Oh my calves are killing me," Emily said.

"Those heels would not help," Mia said gesturing to Emily's high heeled shoes.

"Yes, they're new," Emily said and noticed that Mia had her finger in a small clay pot.

"May I?" asked Mia.

"Sure," nodded Emily.

Mia crouched down behind Emily's legs and started to rub the ointment in. It smelt like menthol and clove. Emily felt the heat on her legs immediately.

"It generates quite a bit of heat doesn't it?" Emily said as Mia massaged the ointment into Emily's calves.

"It's just getting started," Mia said.

Emily could feel the heat seep through her skin and deep into the muscles of her leg. She no longer thought about the aching calves but now was more concerned about the hot sensation on her skin.

"What is in this?" Emily asked.

"I don't know but I have been buying it off my man for years. It's very safe. The heat will pass," Mia said.

Emily's soreness in her calves just melted away leaving a pleasant tingling sensation on her skin.

"That is good," Emily said.

"Anywhere else?" Mia enquired.

"Oh, my lower back but don't worry about it," Emily said.

"No, it's no bother," Mia said, "Slip your dress off and fold it over the deck chair.

"Oh no. That's fine," Emily said, slightly embarrassed.

"Don't worry. I often sun bake out here. No one can see us unless they are looking at us with high powered binoculars from another building."

Emily looked around and saw no signs of anyone else around in the neighboring buildings.

"OK then," Emily said and slipped off her dress.

"Your abs are amazing," Mia said.

"Yes, I didn't even know I had abs until recently," Emily said.

"Hold onto the railing," Mia said.

Emily held onto the railing and looked at the vast distance to the ground, "Whoa."

Mia put her finger in the clay pot and rubbed both her hands with the ointment and started to massage Emily's lower back.

"I have to admit that feels amazing," Emily said.

"My pleasure," said Mia.

Emily could feel all the pain and tightness from her lower back melt away and felt an overwhelming sense of lightness like she could just float off the balcony up into the air.

"Would you like a drink?" Mia asked, "Mineral water?"

"That would be nice," said Emily.

"Just let the ointment dry before putting your dress back on," said Mia, "It can leave a slight stain unless you let it completely dry into the skin."

"Sure," said Emily sitting on the deck chair with her legs crossed.

Mia left and returned with two glasses of water and sat next to Emily.

"Emily, can I tell you something?" Mia asked.

"Sure," said Emily.

"You look amazing."

"Thank you," Emily said smiling.

"Would it be OK if I kissed you?"

Emily blushed. She had known Mia for so many years and she had never indicated any attraction to her before or even that she liked women.

"I'm sorry if I have embarrassed you. Please forgive me," Mia said.

"Sure," Emily said shyly.

"Sure – you forgive me?" Mia asked.

"Sure, you can kiss me," said Emily.

Mia smiled with a twinkle in her eye and maintaining eye contact gently pressed her lips against Emily's lips.

Mia's lips were so soft, much softer than Jay's lips, which were strong and muscular. Mia's kiss was soft and warm like she was melting into Emily.

Mia then kissed along Emily's neck, tentatively at first and then more confidently, kissing over each of Jay's love bites. Mia then reached behind and unhooked Emily's bra, laying it on a small table next to them. Mia stroked Emily's breasts. They must still have had traces of ointment on them because Emily felt heat streamlining onto her breasts from Mia's hands. Mia gently stroked each of Emily's nipples as she kissed Emily's face and neck. Mia then stroked the back of Emily's head and neck, while kissing Emily closely.

Mia then pulled at Emily's panties with both hands and Emily sat off the chair slightly to allow them to be removed.

"Move forward slightly," said Mia breathlessly.

Emily moved to the edge of her chair and Mia then used her hands to pull Emily's legs apart, looking at Emily's sex in the warm sun.

"Beautiful," Mia said, before bending down to lick Emily's clit, while playing with her breasts with one hand.

Mia licked up and down between Emily's legs, exploring each crease and fold with her tongue, sending Emily into paroxysms of pleasure as she held onto Mia's shoulders, more and more tightly.

"Oh." Emily sighed as she fell over the cliff of pleasure, the sun dazzlingly bright.

CHAPTER 8. ROAD

Emily lay on her bed at night thinking of her two lovers – her personal trainer, Jay and her best friend, Mia. She felt a guilty pleasure in having sex with both of them and also regret about crossing lines she probably should not have crossed. Pleasure prevailed over the guilt and Emily stroked herself as she thought about each lover, images of both of them flashing through her mind.

Jay's father was a mechanic and loved repairing and renovating old Chevy trucks and had given one to Jay as a birthday present. Jay had suggested that Emily join him for a drive out of New York to Eagle Rock Reservation.

Emily was impressed by the immaculate blue Chevy with chrome exhaust and the modern refit of the cabin with air conditioning and a modern stereo system with Bluetooth, satnav and all the latest technology.

Emily wound down the window and the wind rushed through her hair as Drake pounded from the stereo system.

Jay drove the car off the main road down a fire break and parked the Chevy next to the forest.

"Do you know deer and bears live in this forest?" Jay asked.

"I do. Amazing that they live so close to the city," Emily said.

"Hey, come and have a look what I have under the tarpaulin in the tray," Jay said gesturing for Emily to join him in the back of the Chevy.

Once they were both standing outside the tray of the Chevy, Jay pulled the tarpaulin back to reveal a black toolbox.

"Oh, a box," said Emily.

Jay smirked, "OK wise guy, look inside the box."

Emily opened the toolbox and found it contained a large assortment of handcuffs, gags, sex toys, and even lingerie. Emily put one item after another down on the tray of the Chevy.

"I don't even know what most of this stuff is. Where did you get it?" Emily asked.

"I saw the Pleasure Chest was having a sale and so I just piled a heap of stuff into my shopping basket. I thought you would like it," said Jay sheepishly.

Emily smiled and held up a little wheel with spikes on it and spun it with her finger and they both laughed.

"Hey, I have something in mind," Jay said.

"Sure," replied Emily.

"You know how much I love seeing your body."

Emily nodded.

"Well I think you would look amazing lying on the bonnet of the Chevy," Jay said, "Tied to the bonnet – my beautiful hood ornament."

"That sounds like something that will get us arrested," Emily laughed.

"Only if we get caught," Jay laughed.

"You don't know me well enough yet. I always get caught. I get away with nothing."

"Yeah well, you're with me now. I'm like Teflon – nothing sticks to me," Jay said.

"Well hopefully your Teflon neutralizes my habit of always getting into trouble whenever I slightly step out of line," Emily said.

"I'm sure it will. Let's give it a try," Jay said.

"OK. But if we get caught…" Emily said but Jay put a finger to her lip to stop Emily speaking. Emily kissed it and sucked it with a wicked grin.

"You are the hottest, most crazy girlfriend I have ever had," Jay said.

Emily smiled and went over to a grassed area where there was a picnic table made of wood and peeled off her top revealing a black bra covering her pale freckled skin.

Emily wiggled her hips as she slid her shorts down her long legs.

She then came over and bent over in front of Jay and moved her bottom up and down against his crotch like a stripper giving a lap dance.

"Girl, where did you learn these moves?" Jay asked.

"Music videos," Emily giggled.

"You have some mighty fine moves," Jay said, feeling himself become firmer against his shorts.

Emily moved in very close and ground her panty clad bottom into Jay's crotch. Jay placed his hands on each side of Emily's hips. She was so smooth and soft.

"Stay there," Jay said as he ran two fingers up and down between Emily's legs until the panties became damp. Emily moaned with pleasure before her legs buckled and she fell to the ground on her hands and knees.

"Oh, Jay, please take me," Emily said, stroking between her legs herself.

"What was that?" Jay asked mischievously.

Emily rubbed herself with more fervor and said breathlessly, "Take me, Jay. Please take me."

Jay reached over and grabbed something from the toolbox. Emily continued to rub herself as she felt something cold and sharp against her buttock.

Emily turned as Jay lifted up the band of her panties and started to cut them open with some shiny silver scissors then he ripped them off her bottom until Emily was bare-assed and almost dripping in anticipation.

Jay then cut Emily's bra strap so it fell to the ground.

"Put your hands behind your back," Jay commanded.

As soon as Emily had done so, Jay slipped a handcuff around each hand and secured Emily's hands together behind her back then lowered Emily down so that her head and chest were pressed against the grass and her bottom was pointing up to the sky.

"Those bent knee deadlifts are really working for you, Emily. Your bottom is magnificent," Scott said.

Emily would have replied but she had a faceful of grass.

Jay pulled his shorts quickly down with one hand and held Emily's hip with the other hand. His erection pressed hard against his taut stomach like the branch of a tree. He pressed it gently at Emily's opening, teasing her with a gentle action in and out of her, edging in slowly bit by bit. It almost did not seem physically possible but soon he was halfway into Emily, her body slightly wiggling as he penetrated her a slightly more deeply, Emily's face and breasts pushed against the grass. Jay could feel that Emily was on the verge of coming but did not want to end now. He slowly withdrew, causing Emily to sigh in frustration.

"Emily, let's go to the tray of the Chevy. I've got a blanket there," Jay said.

Jay walked to the Chevy, his erection larger than ever, as he thought about all the fun and games they could have in the woods. Emily followed behind, her arms tightly restricted behind her back.

Jay spread out the blanket at the back of the Chevy tray and sat down and looked at his erection and then at Emily. That was all the instruction Emily needed as she leaned down to take Jay's erection in her mouth.

Emily's head bobbed up and down upon the top of Jay's erection as she leaned over with her arms behind her back. Jay ran his hands through Emily's hair as she tried to take more and more of him in her mouth and throat.

"That's it," said Jay, "OK, now kiss me."

Emily stood straight and explored Jay's mouth with her tongue. Jay loved the feeling of Emily's tongue sliding against his as his hands explored Emily's butt and between her legs.

When their lips finally parted, Emily inhaled deeply and Jay stood up, his erection moving into Emily and she had to stand high on the top of her toes to accommodate all of him. Jay then lifted Emily by her hips as she wrapped her legs around him, her arms still bound behind her back, and he penetrated her even more deeply than before, gravity bringing her deeper and deeper onto him. Emily slipped her tongue back into Jay's mouth. She passionately kissed him as she felt all consumed by him as their bodies ground together.

Two hikers, a man, and a woman, both bird watchers, walked along the road, the man staring at the two young lovers making out so blatantly in broad daylight. The woman elbowed the man in the ribs and his stare was broken.

The woman said, "Hey, eyes to the front please, mister."

Jay and Emily were too lost in the moment to even notice them as they both moaned together in pleasure

As Jay lowered Emily to the ground she felt his come dribble down her leg as she caught her breath.

Jay looked at Emily; her skin was beautifully flushed red like she was in heat.

"Wow," Jay said.

"Yes, indeed, wow," said Emily.

"Hey, I'm not finished with you yet," Jay said.

"Well, unless you are a miracle worker, you really are finished," Emily said nodding at Jay's come on her leg.

Jay took the key to the handcuffs and unlocked Emily's hands. There were red rings around where the handcuffs had been. Jay squeezed massage oil onto his hands and massaged it into Emily's wrists, "This should help."

"They're fine," said Emily.

"Now Emily, I want you to take this oil and go over to that picnic table over there and lie down on it. Then spread your legs apart and pour the oil all over your body. Close your eyes and massage it all over your skin," Jay said.

"Okay," Emily said, feeling herself getting aroused again at the thought of being on display for Jay.

"Then masturbate yourself until you scream with pleasure," Jay said.

"You don't ask for much," Emily said cheekily.

Jay playfully slapped Emily's butt as she walked towards the picnic table with the massage oil. She lay down upon it with her legs facing Jay. She giggled as she spread her legs for him and looked over to him.

Jay licked his lips as if he was looking at his Thanksgiving lunch and amazingly he was starting to get hard again.

Emily closed her eyes and poured the massage oil on her breasts and then her legs and between her legs. The oil had a rich musky smell and warmed her skin.

There was a light breeze brushing over Emily's body as she started to massage the oil into her breasts with one hand on each breast, moving in concentric circles. Emily then massaged her stomach and the top of her thighs. Her clitoris was still too sensitive to touch but she got a pleasant sensation from stroking her labia and then started to stimulate her clit by sandwiching it between her labia and gently pulsing with her hands.

Jay approached Emily who still had her eyes closed and stroked her cheek with the back of his hand, "Come on baby, I know you can do this for me."

Emily pulsed her fingers harder while Jay pulled and stroked her nipples.

"Come on Emily, you can do this. I want multiple orgasms from you," Jay said as Emily went at it even harder, wanting to please her personal trainer.

Emily arched her back and her breathing went quiet.

"That's it, Emily. Good work," Jay said.

Emily felt a ripple of pleasure wash through her body until it dominated every cell of her and she screamed with pleasure. All the wild animals in the woods were quiet for a moment as the scream echoed through the woods.

Emily opened her eyes and saw Jay staring into them.

"You did good, Emily," Jay said as he smiled from ear to ear.

CHAPTER 9. WEIGHTS

Mia was initially very happy that Emily and Jay had got together. She had wanted Emily to have an adventure with Jay – have her toes curled, build some confidence and then move on, preferably with someone wealthy and charming from work.

Now she could not even manage to get Jay on the telephone to book a workout with him – his message bank was constantly on. He did not return her calls and she would sometimes see them walking arm in arm along the sidewalk.

What is that saying? Be careful what you wish for. Mia realized that she was now jealous of Emily's relationship with Jay. Despite being attractive and vivacious Mia was having trouble getting a boyfriend and was not only lonely but very sexually frustrated. Mia felt like Emily and Jay owed her for her setting them up together. She felt like it was time for them to settle the account.

Mia's plan was quite simple. She invited Emily for a gym session after work booked Jay for a personal training session as well.

"Hello ladies," said Jay smiling at Mia and Emily who were both lifting heavy weights.

"Jay!" Emily said with an immediate blush coming over her face.

"Hello best personal trainer in all of New York," said Mia.

"If you say so, Mia," said Jay.

"You know it's true," said Mia.

"Well it could be I have the best students in New York," Jay said.

"Hey, Jay. Could you help Emily and me with some yoga positions up in the yoga room?" Mia asked.

"No problem," said Jay.

The yoga room was empty. The last yoga class had finished an hour ago.

"What position did you want to try, Mia?" asked Jay.

"The puppy dog stretch," Mia said.

"Lengthens the spine and calms the mind," Jay said, "OK well get onto all fours the two of you."

Mia and Emily both moved down to the floor and got onto all fours.

"Your shoulders should be above your wrists and your hips above your knees. Walk your hands forward and curl your toes under," Jay said, "As you exhale, move your buttocks halfway back toward your heels. Keep your arms active; don't let your elbows touch the ground."

Mia and Emily competed to see who could get into position the best.

"Now drop your forehead to the floor or to a blanket and let your neck relax. Keep a slight curve in your lower back. To feel a nice long stretch in your spine, press the hands down and stretch through the arms while pulling your hips back toward your heels," said Jay, admiring the shapely bottom of each of the women.

"How's that?" asked Mia.

"Very good," said Jay, "Breath into your back, feeling the spine lengthen in both directions. Hold for thirty seconds, then release your buttocks down onto your heels."

"It's quite hot in here tonight. Would either of you mind if I removed my top?" Mia asked.

"Ahh... Be my guest," said Jay wondering what Mia was up to.

Mia stood up and peeled her top off and then her bra.

Jay could not help but look at Mia's pert breasts.

Emily felt an immediate pang of jealousy.

"I'm hot too," Emily said, peeling off her top and bra as well then pulling off her shorts and panties.

"You ladies are lit," Jay said, "Hey this is kinda fantasy of mine."

"What?" asked Mia.

"Well to have two lovely ladies at the same time," Jay said.

"That is kind of presumptuous of you, Mr. Jay. You know you are working on my dime," Mia said.

"That makes it all the more wicked," said Jay.

"Well tell us how this fantasy goes, Mr. Jay," said Mia.

"Let's see. Well how about you give Emily a kiss," Jay said.

Mia smiled at Emily and pecked her on the cheek.

"Nah, not like that. On the lips," said Jay.

Mia leaned in and kissed Emily softly on the lips.

"OK well keep doing that. That was good and Emily put your hand down Mia's panties and stroke her – you know," Jay said.

Mia leaned in and kissed Emily again so that their lips locked and Emily snaked her hand down the front of Mia's panties until her fingers found the delicate crease of her labia and the moist center between her legs and started to stroke her.

"Wow. This is kinda hot," said Jay, "OK Emily – pull Mia's panties down with your teeth."

Emily bent down and held up the band of Mia's panties so she could hold it with her teeth and then pulled the panties down with her mouth holding onto them as she bent down to lower them to the floor.

"OK. Now face each other and interlock your legs," Jay said.

Soon both women were seated on the ground, their legs interlocked and their vulvas pressed against each other.

"Now grind," said Jay.

Emily and Mia then started grinding together as they kissed each other, releasing soft moans.

Jay then started to strip. It was clear that he had been aroused by the two women on the floor. He beckoned them towards him with his index finger.

Mia and Emily crawled over to him, already both dripping wet with desire.

"Emily take me in your mouth," said Jay, "And Mia you can lick my nipples."

Jay released a sigh as their lips and tongue made contact with his muscular body. Emily's mouth slithered up and down Jay's black shaft, taking even more of it than she had in the past. Emily's eyes had a look of deep concentration, focusing on Jay's pleasure, teasing the tip of his penis with her tongue, totally dedicated to his pleasure. Not to be outdone, Mia was sensuously licking one of Jay's nipples and then the other.

The women teased Jay until he closed his eyes lost in pleasure.

How could I escalate this even further? wondered Jay – *I know.*

Jay opened his eyes again and had to fight the urge to ejaculate, looking at the two beautiful women so dedicated to his pleasure.

"Wooh, easy ladies. I don't want to come too quickly," Jay said, "But thank you. You are amazing – my beautiful Emily and your beautiful friend."

Emily and Mia both looked at Jay, wondering what he was going to say next.

"Now ladies, assume the yoga position again," Jay said.

Mia and Jay quickly got into the puppy dog stretch position again next to each other so that Jay was presented with each of their shapely bottoms side by side to each other, high up in the air.

Jay bent down and drove his tongue into Emily, darting in and out with his tongue with a strong intensity while using his hand to stimulate Mia at the same time.

Both Emily and Mia breathed rapidly as they moaned, their chests rising and falling quickly.

Jay then stood up and penetrated Emily deeply with his erection, a testament to the degree of arousal she felt. While easing himself in and out of Emily, Jay continued to use his hands to stimulate Mia, alternating between penetrating her with his fingers to rubbing her clit.

The sound of moaning echoed throughout the yoga room. Emily closed her eyes as she could feel herself reaching a climax but did not want the delicious sensations to end. Emily's eyes then opened wide as if she was startled as a wave of pleasure seized her body.

"Jay, that was amazing," Emily said as Jay withdrew from her, still swollen with desire.

"Emily, I want you to help me with Mia. Go to my gym bag over there," Jay said as he entered Mia now, Mia feeling the fullness of Jay within her.

Emily went to Jay's gym bag and had a look inside. There was nothing of note – just Jay's towel, a change of clothes, shoes, some hand weights and a jump rope.

"Get the rope and bring it over here," Jay said while thrusting into Mia from behind.

"Now bring the end of the rope between your legs and just hold the handle of the rope up between your legs," Jay said.

Emily did as she was asked. The rope was somewhat itchy between her legs but the handle smooth.

"Now stand in front of Mia. That's right. And Mia, you such on the handle like it was a cock," said Jay.

Mia was in no state to respond as she was on the verge of coming.

Emily stood there for a second and slightly shrugged her shoulders then Mia moved her head from the floor and wrapped her lips around the handle of the jump rope and mouthed up and down the handle.

"Not bad," said Emily, not knowing why she said it.

Moments later Jay let out a long sigh as he climaxed.

"Emily, can you finish Mia for me?" asked Jay.

Mia moved around behind Mia and used the handle of the rope as a dildo, rubbing it up and down between Mia's legs as Mia dropped her head to the floor again.

Emily then flicked her tongue on either side of Mia's clit and alternating using the handle to penetrate Mia.

Suddenly Jay spanked Mia's buttock with his hand.

Mia did not know why but that sent her into a state of bliss.

Jay continued to stimulate Mia's clit with her tongue as Jay spanked Mia again.

When Jay spanked Mia a third time Mia released a small cry of pleasure.

CHAPTER 9. HARD

The following day Jay had to attend college to attend a class. Emily, who had spent the night with Jay, had a day off work and so decided to accompany Jay to the college.

They caught the subway together. Jay read some of his sports science textbook on the train. Emily looked at the complex equations in the book and said, "That looks hard."

"Not as hard as you make me," Jay whispered in Emily's ear making her giggle.

At the college, Emily snuck into the class with Jay. The lecturer was in his forties, a former professional basketball coach and somewhat of a tough guy. Emily found that there was a certain level of aggression in some of the comments the lecturer made about the psychology of sporting success.

After the lecture, Jay said, "Come on Emily. Let me introduce you to the Prof."

"No, that's OK," Emily said.

"Come on, his bark is worse than his bite," Jay said.

"Prof, this is my girlfriend Emily," said Jay who was shaking hands with the lecturer.

"Pleased to meet you, Emily," the lecturer said.

"I told Emily you were the head coach for the New York Knicks back in the day."

"Oh that's ancient history now, Jay," said the lecturer.

"Any chance you could show Emily your signed game ball?" Jay asked.

"Sure," said the lecturer.

Jay and the lecturer chatted as they all walked to his office.

"You two have a seat, while I get the ball from my locker. Did you want a Coke? If so, help yourself there is a bar fridge under my desk."

"He seems cool," said Emily, "Different on a personal level to how he seemed in that lecture."

"He just went into coach mode," said Jay, "Hey you know what would be cool?"

"What?" asked Jay.

"Having sex on the Prof's desk before he gets back," sniggered Jay.

"Are you mad? Do you want to get kicked out of college? He'll be back any second."

Jay then discreetly guided Emily's hand over to Jay's rock hard penis which was peaking from the top of his trousers.

"This is obviously turning you on being in the Prof's office," Emily said rubbing him slightly with her hand.

"Emily, just take your top off while you do that," said Jay, "Come on he'll be a while yet. His locker is on the other side of the quadrangle."

Emily gave a doubtful smile then pulled her top over her head, leaving her in a black bra, a short skirt, and heels. She unzipped Jay's trousers and took his erection in her hand, pumping him with her fist.

"That's great baby," Jay whispered.

Emily found the look of abandon on Jay's face and the sense of danger strangely arousing.

"Oh I'm almost there," Jay said, his cock now standing perfectly vertical, "Pull down your panties and lean over the desk over there."

"Hey he'll be back any second," Emily said.

"I'll be quick," said Jay, "Come on Emily."

Emily approached the desk, pulled her panties down to her ankles and leaned over the Prof's desk with her legs as far apart as the panties would allow.

Without warning, Jay picked up the Prof's ruler and smacked it across Emily's buttocks.

"What was that for?" Emily said turning around.

"I thought you liked that," Jay said.

"I did," said Emily, turning to face the wall again.

The force of Jay's penetration lifted Emily off the desk.

"You are so tight," said Jay.

A powerful moan came from Emily as inch after inch slid into Emily until Jay's entire shaft had been swallowed up by her. With each thrust, Emily wriggled with fullness and pleasure.

Jay pounded Emily against the desk, the force of his thrusts made Emily's body rock back and forth, moving in and out of her. Then the stimulation became too much for either of them to handle as Jay pulsed into Emily as she moaned loudly with pleasure, the danger and vibration causing one of the most powerful orgasms she had ever experienced.

Wave after wave of pleasure fell upon them as they both felt lighter than air. Jay continued to ride Emily until he was spent. Both of them could scarcely breathe as Jay kissed Emily's mouth, their tongues dancing in desire.

Emily brought her finger up to Jay's lips and looked at him and nodded. She then discretely wiped her legs with a tissue and pulled her panties up over her bottom. Jay tucked himself back into his trousers and wiped the sweat from his brow. Jay then went to the bar fridge and gave each of them a Coke. It felt to both of them like the nectar of the Gods. Every inch of them still tingled with electricity.

When the Prof knocked on the door and entered he said, "Sorry to keep you waiting. I ran into a colleague and got lost track of the time."

"I know the feeling Prof," said Jay.

CHAPTER 10. ORCHIDS

As well as working as a personal trainer Jay was also teaching a class at the local boxing gym, Showdown, which was run by a friend of Jay's nicknamed Wolf. Jay convinced Emily to give it a go and push her workout to a new level.

Showdown was a dark room with forty punching bags, pulsing with club music. Jay had the class alternate between punching the bags and then doing planks and push-ups.

After the class, Jay and Emily went to the change rooms to shower. As Emily was at her locker another woman brushed past her.

"It's pretty intense isn't it," the woman said.

"Yeah, Jay doesn't go by half measures. He's all in," laughed Emily.

"He would make a good drill sergeant."

They both laughed.

"Are you French?" asked Emily.

"Haitian. Hey, my name's Stéphanie."

"Emily."

Stéphanie and Emily shook hands with Stéphanie holding on to Emily's hand longer than is usual. Stéphanie smelt amazing to Emily. The workout had activated Stéphanie's perfume that smelt like tropical orchids in a jungle at night.

"Emily, excuse me for saying but I find you really attractive," said Stéphanie.

"Thank you," Emily said, wondering if she was now giving out some kind of sexual aura.

Stéphanie stared into Emily's eyes and then looked at her lips and slightly leaned in. This was so unusual but so intoxicating, thought Emily who leaned slightly closer to Stéphanie.

"I love your freckles," said Stéphanie.

"I love your dark skin," said Emily.

Stéphanie moved so close to Emily that she could feel Stéphanie's breathe on her cheek.

"Do you have freckles all over?" asked Stéphanie.

"Just where…" said Emily before Stéphanie cut her off mid-sentence with a kiss that seemed to go on forever then Stéphanie's hands move down Emily's thighs, and finally Stéphanie slipped her hands down Emily's yoga pants and started gently massaging her clit. It felt so good to Emily that she gasped.

When Emily came to her senses again she looked around the change room to see if anyone else was watching them.

"We should take this somewhere private," said Stéphanie.

"Where?" whispered Emily.

"Well, I need a shower. What about you?" said Stéphanie stripping off her gym wear and leaving a trail of clothes to the shower cubicle, her body gorgeous in every detail.

Emily shyly undressed with a fluffy white towel around herself and then walked over to the showers.

Hot steam was emanating from the shower cubicle Stéphanie was in. She was singing some beautiful song in French that sounded like a lullaby.

As Emily approached the cubicle door opened and Stéphanie wrapped her arms around Emily, her towel falling to the ground and they were wrapped in a naked embrace, Stéphanie's body dressed in steam, warm and inviting.

Emily and Stéphanie consumed each other with their mouths, their tongues intertwined and their hands exploring each curve of each other. Stéphanie then kissed along Emily's neck, then along the side of each breast, then in a circle around her stomach and then Stéphanie separated Emily's labia to expose the pink orchid within. The shower spray fell upon Emily's flower then Stéphanie probed her deeply with her tongue while stimulating her clitoris with two fingers. Emily threw her head back and moaned as Stéphanie grabbed each of her buttocks and held her close. Stéphanie now was probing Emily deeply with her fingers, curling them up while sucking upon Emily's clit. Emily reached down and caressed and stroked Stéphanie's head.

Stéphanie looked up at Emily whose eyes were closed, lost in the moment. *Now you're mine*, thought Stéphanie.

Emily thought she would faint with pleasure as she came, warm nectar between her legs. Stéphanie stood up and cupped Emily's face with her hands and kissed Emily's mouth, her breath hot and her mouth wet with desire.

When they finally separated to draw breath, Emily asked, "Is there something I can do for you?"

Stéphanie kissed Emily's cheek and said, "Hmm, let me think."

Emily kissed Stéphanie and said, "There must be something."

"I know," said Stéphanie, "I want you to go get your towel but don't dry yourself off. I like you wet. Do you have an iPod?"

"Yes," answered Emily, intrigued by where Stéphanie was going.

"Excellent," said Stéphanie, "Get it from your locker and put on the headphones, put on your favorite music and put it up loud. Then lie down on the towel, legs either side of the bench and make yourself come again. Close your eyes and keep them closed. When you are climaxing I will ask you to do something for me."

Stéphanie looked into Emily's eyes and Emily nodded.

As Emily left the shower, Stéphanie smacked Emily's bottom playfully and then followed Emily out.

Emily bent over and picked up the towel from the floor then went to her locker and got her iPod as instructed. She put the headphones into her ears and turned on her favorite classical track, Beethoven's ninth symphony and turned it up loud. She then draped the white towel over the bench which was in the center of the room between the two walls of lockers.

Emily then went to the door of the change rooms and peaked out. The hallway was empty.

Emily then lay down upon the towel, resting a leg on either side of the bench. With her legs splayed she stroked herself in time with the music. Emily then closed her eyes.

Stéphanie dressed in a skirt and blouse, keeping her eyes on Emily. After a minute or so three women came into the change rooms. They were immediately taken aback by Emily, so wantonly displaying herself in the middle of the change room.

Stéphanie smiled at the women and tilted her head towards Emily and raised her eyebrows.

"She's was doing that when I came in," said Stéphanie.

"She looks like she's having a good time," said the first woman who watched Emily's chest rise and fall while one of Emily's hands was stroking her nipples while the other one was buried deep between her legs.

"What a tramp," said the second woman sniggering.

"She's quite sexy," said the third woman.

"Touch her," said Stéphanie, "I dare you."

"I'm not touching that," said the second woman.

"She doesn't look like she needs any help," said the first woman.

"It's her fantasy," said Stéphanie, "She wants you to see her. She wants you to touch her."

"Total strangers?" asked the second woman.

"Just touch her leg and you will see," said Stéphanie.

The second woman lightly touched the top of one of Emily's thighs. Emily immediately purred with pleasure.

"What a freak," said the second woman.

"Twist her nipple," said Stéphanie.

"What?" asked the second woman.

"I'll do it," said the third woman, stepping forward and holding Emily's left nipple between her thumb and finger and twisting the nipple lightly.

"Oh," Emily moaned.

"What a tramp," said the second woman.

"My turn," said the first woman stepping forward and brushing her hand up and down Emily's thighs."

"Oh," Emily moaned again.

"Does she desire everyone who touches her?" asked the first woman.

"Yes," said Stéphanie, "And you know what she likes doing the best?"

"I can't wait," said the second woman.

"Eating women out," said Stéphanie.

The women all giggled.

"Don't laugh," said Stéphanie, "She's very talented. Best tongue in New York."

The women giggled again and Stéphanie kissed Emily on the lips then moved her fingers to Emily's lips and then into Emily's mouth who then sucked upon them while still stroking up and down between her legs, pinching her labia together to stimulate her clit.

Stéphanie studied the intense look on Emily's face and knew she was a short time away from climaxing.

"Don't you want to have the orgasm of your lifetime?" asked Stéphanie.

"This is crazy," said the second woman.

"I'll try it," said the third woman, yanking up her work skirt and pulling down her panties.

"OK," said Stéphanie, "Now stand astride her face and wait until I tell you to lower yourself down."

"Darlene, you are wild," said the first woman and they all laughed.

"Well I don't want to die wondering," said the third woman.

Stéphanie kissed and stroked Emily's cheek and neck. This was enough to send Emily into paroxysms of pleasure. Stéphanie then nodded to Darlene who lowered her pussy onto Emily's face. Emily immediately licked and slurped the length of Darlene's labia and then probed between them with her tongue, finding the tip of her opening and alternated between sucking and licking Darlene's clit.

Darlene and Emily moaned in unison while the other three women looked on in fascination. Darlene was soon riding Emily's mouth like a horse, bucking forwards and backward and grinding into Emily's face. The two other women stroked Emily's breasts and pulled her nipples while Stéphanie kissed Emily's mouth, swallowing Emily's orgasm when it came.

When Emily finally exited the change rooms she found Jay waiting for her.

"I was getting worried about you. Thought you might have passed out in there," said Jay.

"I almost did," said Emily with a cheeky smile.

"Shall we grab a drink at the juice bar?" asked Jay.

"Sure," said Emily.

The juice bar was at the front of the gym with a polished concrete floor and large industrial windows.

"Hey Jay," Wolf called out from across the room as he entered arm in arm with Stéphanie.

CHAPTER 11. WOLF

Wolf invited Emily and Jay to join Stéphanie and him for an evening of nightclubbing.

At first, it was quite strange for Emily as Stéphanie and she kept exchanging knowing looks and Stéphanie had quite a superior and bossy attitude towards her. Later after a number of cocktails both of them relaxed and even danced together when Emily's favorite dance track was played at the club they were in.

Wolf and Jay sat at the bar watching their girlfriends dance together.

"You like Emily?" asked Jay.

"She's not your usual type," said Wolf.

"She's amazing," said Jay.

"In bed?" asked Wolf watching Stéphanie and Emily grind their hips together on the dancefloor.

"Frankly yes," said Jay.

"What's she into?" asked Wolf.

"What have you got?"

"It's like that is it," Wolf laughed, "Find yourself a freak and never let go of her, my friend."

"I have to admit the sex is amazing but I'm not a one girl man – you know that."

"Can I tap that?" asked Wolf.

Jay thought for a second, "You know what would really do it for her?"

"Do tell brother," said Wolf.

"A kinky foursome where she served all of us," Jay said into Wolf's ear.

Wolf guffawed with laughter.

"Well, you have come to the right man. Kinkiness is my middle name," Wolf said, not caring who heard it.

When Stéphanie and Emily returned from the dancefloor they quickly knocked down two ice-cold cocktails each, laughing at each other's dumb jokes. Jay and Wolf joined in and soon it seemed that the group was having the best time out of anyone in the club.

Wolf and Jay stood very close to the woman, closing in on them until they were practically touching them. Wolf paid so much attention to Emily that Stéphanie started to get jealous.

Wolf was a former quarterback and college boxing champion, lean and muscled with a handsome face, dark and chiseled. Stéphanie and Wolf had been together for a year. Even though they had an open relationship Stéphanie could not stand it if Wolf started showing too much interest in another woman.

"What's say you and Jay, join Steph and me for cocktails at my crib. I live just around the corner from her. I have amazing views of the water," said Wolf.

"Just one cocktail and then we better get home," said Emily, "I've got work tomorrow."

"I empathize," said Wolf who had never worked in an office in his life.

After leaving the club the group caught a taxi even though it was only a short distance to Wolf's building. Wolf kept flirting with Emily in the taxi, making Stéphanie fume. When Stéphanie was not looking Wolf even slipped his hand up Emily's dress and felt her thigh.

The view from Wolf's apartment was amazing. He looked over the deep blue of the Hudson River, the skyscraper lights twinkling over the water.

Wolf's had decorated his walls with extra-large black and white photographs of boxing greats like Muhammad Ali and Mike Tyson, throwing punches. The group settled into a large black plush corner lounge suite where Wolf served them drinks from his bar.

Both Jay and Wolf complemented and flirted with Emily in a competitive way, both vying for her attention. They were both letting

Emily know they wanted her. Stéphanie felt like she was not even in the room.

Stéphanie puts on some music – something chilled and bass heavy and goes and drinks her drink on the balcony overlooking the water.

Jay nods to Wolf in the direction of Stéphanie and Wolf goes and joins her on the balcony and wraps his arm around her, holds her close and kisses her.

"You OK, Steph?" Wolf asked.

"Yeah, baby," Stéphanie replied.

On the lounge, Jay ran both his hands up along Emily's legs all the way to the top of her thighs and kissed her softly on her lips.

"You look amazing," Jay said.

"You too," said Emily.

Jay then reached the top of Emily's panties and pulled them down along her legs and over her black high heeled shoes.

"We don't need these do we, Emily?" Jay whispered in Emily's ear.

"No sir," said Emily kissing Jay's cheek softly, like an opening flower.

Jay then buried his face between Emily's legs, Emily leaning back against the soft black leather of the couch. Emily closed her eyes as Jay expertly caressed her labia and clit with his tongue in a sturdy circular motion. Jay slipped his hands under Emily's pale buttocks to move her closer to him.

Emily's moaning caught Wolf's attention on the balcony and he and Stéphanie re-entered the apartment, watching Jay's technique.

"Not bad brother," said Wolf.

"Me next," said Stéphanie.

Jay looked up at them and said with a chuckle, "Can't a brother get some privacy over here."

"My apartment, brother," replied Wolf, "Come on, give a brother some of that."

Wolf put his hand on Jay's shoulder and Jay stood up.

Stéphanie yanked down her panties and threw them at Jay, sat on a lounge chair and splayed her legs, "Come over here, big boy."

Wolf kissed Emily's inner thighs.

"I love your pussy," said Wolf, pulling the labia apart with his fingers, "It's a work of art. Everything that Stéphanie told me."

Emily blushed at the stranger looking at her so intimately and at the thought of what Stéphanie had told Wolf.

"Don't believe everything Stéphanie says," said Emily.

"Don't I know it," said Wolf who then buried his tongue deep within the folds between Emily's legs.

Emily looked over at Jay who was doing the same thing to Stéphanie who was looking at Emily and smiled a somewhat superior smile then rolled her eyes back as if she was having an incredible orgasm. *Well maybe she was*, thought Emily.

Emily ground herself against Wolf's tongue, riding his face slowly and deeply.

Wolf then unbuttoned Emily's blouse and unhooked her bra.

"Very dainty," said Wolf examining it.

Wolf then ran his tongue over Emily's nipples and touched her everywhere else until she positively buzzed with excitement.

Wolf then got up from the floor, unzipped his jeans and sat naked on the sofa with his legs apart. He was already half erect and had a python between his legs. He smiled at Wolf. He always loved seeing that look of nervous excitement when women saw his penis.

Emily moved up off the sofa and bent down and started moving her mouth up and down over the head of Wolf's cock. Jay also stood up and turned around to see Emily bent over Wolf, her legs impossibly long in high black heels and her bare buttocks peeking from beneath her skirt as she leaned over.

Jay then felt the warm wet mouth of Stéphanie upon his erection. She wrapped her legs around him and was bobbing her head up and down upon him, making loud slurping noises.

Not to be outdone, Emily pushed herself to take Wolf deeper within her mouth and throat.

"Jay, your girlfriend is the best," said Wolf.

This prompted Stéphanie to work even harder at getting Jay off, sucking his balls and stroking between Jay's legs while sucking and licking his erection.

"Jay, get over here a minute," said Wolf.

"Yeah man," said Jay.

"Your girl's pussy needs attention while she does this," said Wolf.

Jay looked over to Emily madly sucking upon Wolf.

"Steph, baby girl, you come over here too. I got something I want you to do too," said Wolf, somewhat breathlessly.

Jay walked over to Emily, lifted her skirt and penetrated her slightly then with each thrust went deeper until he was so deep into her that he almost lifted her feet off the floor. Emily murmured slightly but did not stop sucking and in fact sucked with greater intensity than before as she felt herself start to edge towards orgasm. Wolf grinned from ear to ear.

"Steph, unbutton my shirt and suck my nipples baby doll," said Wolf.

Stéphanie slightly raised her eyebrows but walked over to Wolf and did as instructed, unbuttoning Wolf's shirt and leaned over him to suck his nipples while he played with her breasts.

"Jay, give Emily's ass some attention now," said Wolf.

Jay licked his fingers so that they glistened with saliva and then ran them down between Emily's buttocks and massaged the entrance to Emily's ass while continuing to thrust into her vagina.

Emily was impossibly tight but he managed to ease one finger into Emily and moved it in and out of her as he thrust into her with his penis below.

"Emily, you are amazing," said Wolf, "Now you come and sit down upon this," said Wolf pointing to his penis that now stood high and proud like a totem pole.

Emily looked up and then wiped her mouth with her hand. She then turned around to face Jay and smiled at him as she slightly lowered herself onto Wolf until the tip of his penis was just resting on her anus.

"Steph, can you help baby doll," said Wolf.

Steph put her hand on Jay's chest and smiled, "Excuse me, big boy," and then started to suck and lick Emily's clit while masturbating Wolf's penis and pushing Emily slightly further down upon it.

Emily wriggled with each downward movement until Wolf's penis was about an inch into her.

"Jay, now you do Emily from the front while I do her from the back," Wolf said.

Jay grabbed under Emily's buttocks and lifted her up slightly as he penetrated her vagina and then lowered her down again so that Wolf penetrated her from behind.

"Oh," said Emily.

"Steph, I want you to spank Jay's butt until he is doing it right," said Wolf.

Stéphanie had a wicked grin on her face as she smacked her hand against Jay's muscular buttocks as he pushed in and out of Emily.

Stéphanie then got behind Jay and thrust her body behind Jay, stroking his chest from behind and bumping into him as he thrust into Emily.

CHAPTER 12. EMOJI

At work the next day, Emily found it hard to concentrate sitting at her work station. Her mind kept thinking of the night before and the mind-blowing orgasm she had experienced with Jay and his two friends.

Instead of working, she found herself checking her telephone to see if there had been any messages from Jay. Finally, at 11.30, a text popped up on her telephone from Jay.

"You good?" said the message.

Emily replied with a happy emoji.

Jay sent a crazy emoji with his tongue hanging out in return.

Emily smiled.

"What U doing?" Jay's next message said.

"Meant to be working," replied Emily.

Jay sent back an emoji yawning.

"Touch yourself," Jay texted.

"No," texted Emily in reply.

"U know U want to," texted Jay.

"You'll get me fired," texted Emily.

"Then U can spend more time with me," texted Jay.

That's sweet, thought Emily.

"Go on," texted Jay.

Emily looked around the office. Everyone was quietly working or talking on the telephone. Emily discretely moved her hand to her thigh and moved her hand up and down along it.

"Done," replied Emily.

"Good girl," replied Jay by text, then the following words appeared on Emily's phone, "Take a photo."

Emily looked around the office. Still, no one was paying her attention and her manager was on the far side of the open plan office.

Emily then turned the flash on her telephone off and took a quick selfie, smiling down into the camera. She checked the photo before texting it to Jay.

"Beautiful," replied Jay then texted, "Something more intimate?"

Emily looked around the office again. The coast was still clear. She unbuttoned the first couple of buttons of her blouse and took another selfie, moving her lips together in an air kiss expression. Emily then texted the photo to Jay.

"Getting me hot," texted Jay.

Emily looked around the office again while discretely buttoning up her blouse. She then texted, "Me too."

"Something more?" Jay texted.

Emily looked around. She had heard there may be CCTV cameras somewhere in the office but concluded that this was just talk. No one was looking at her and the manager was still on the other side of the floor.

Emily then moved the camera under her desk and slightly spread her legs to take the next photograph. She looked around the room again before checking the photograph. It was so dark you could barely tell what it showed. Emily decided to text it to Jay anyway.

"Wow," Jay texted back, "What floor U on?"

Emily hesitated before replying. The floor was locked down. You could not even get past the receptionist without a pass. *What the heck*, thought Emily and texted "Level 17, West 45th Street."

"Go to the men's toilet and get lost in the deep end. Will knock twice. Be there is 15."

"What?" Emily texted back, "Are you mad?"

There was no reply. *What do I do now?* thought Emily. She looked at her watch. Jay will never get into the building. She could not help feel slightly aroused by Jay's proposition but also slightly mortified by the thought of one of her co-workers discovering her going into the men's toilet. And what did *get lost in the deep end* mean?

Emily tried to put the text out of her mind but her thoughts kept coming back to it. She decided that she would go to the toilet anyway just before the appointed time. Emily went to the kitchen which was outside the main work area near the lifts and near the male toilets.

"Hi Emily," said a male co-worker who entered the kitchen to get some hot water for his coffee.

"Oh hello," Emily said, slowly drinking her water until the man had left. She then checked the whole area and when she was certain that no one was around, put the glass down and went into the men's toilet area.

It was almost a mirror image to the women's toilet but had a urinal and fewer stalls. Emily quickly made her way into one of the stalls and shut the door so quickly that it slightly banged.

What are you doing Emily? she thought, blood pulsing through her veins.

Emily put the lid of the toilet down and sat there on the toilet. She closed her eyes and thought of Jay and the wild adventures she had the day before. Emily spread her legs slightly and started to stroke herself over her panties, giving herself a pleasant buzz.

The door of the toilet opened suddenly and Emily thought that she could not breathe for a moment before she heard Jay's voice whispering, "Are you there?"

Emily quickly opened the stall door and Emily came over, closed the door and hugged Emily. He held two brown Uber bags which he dropped to the floor.

After they had kissed Emily smiled and said, "How did you get in here?"

"I said I was an Uber Eats driver with a delivery for you," Jay chuckled.

"I will have to give you a substantial tip," said Emily.

"No need I have a substantial tip for you," said Jay.

Emily could feel Jay's erection swelling against her belly.

"Could you not have waited until after work?" Emily said.

"Too far away," said Jay.

"You are going to get me sacked you know that," Emily said.

"Look a session with your personal trainer is a perfectly legitimate way of relieving a little work stress. I should send my bill to your boss. I might just go and find him and have a little word," Jay said pretending to move to leave the cubicle before Emily wrapped her lips around Jay's mouth again.

Jay then reaches up and pulls Emily's panties down and places them on top of the brown bags. He then unzips his trousers and lifts Emily up, who wraps her legs around Jay and rests her back against the wall of the cubicle as Jay edges into her, breathing heavily while Emily softly moans. They both freeze as someone comes into the restroom and try and hold their breath as they listen to a man using the urinal and then washing his hands, whistling while he does so.

As soon as the door closes again, Jay continues thrusting, quickly regaining the strength of his erection as he penetrates Emily even more deeply, their lips locked upon each other, their sounds of pleasure muffled by the other's mouth.

When they had finished Jay decided to take Emily's panties home in one of the brown paper bags as a souvenir.

CHAPTER 14. SHOW

"So what does Wolf's girlfriend do for a job?" asked Emily as she caught the subway with Jay to meet up with them downtown.

"She's a window dresser," said Jay, "And some kind of artist."

"Have you known Wolf long?" asked Emily.

"We played for the same football team. Became buddies then," said Jay.

"I bet you two were party animals," said Emily.

"We were half nerds half jocks, to be honest," said Jay.

"I find that hard to believe," said Emily.

"It's true," said Jay.

Jay and Emily exited the subway and met up with Wolf and Stéphanie in an old school diner. Wolf had his arm around Stéphanie in a booth. A jazz chanteuse crooned over the speakers about a blue moon.

"You are even more beautiful now than you were last time I saw you," said Wolf kissing Emily's hand.

"How's it doin' brother?" Wolf fist pumped Jay.

Stéphanie and Emily air kissed each other.

"So what we doing tonight bro?" asked Jay.

"I was hoping Emily could help me at work tonight," said Stéphanie.

"Yeah whatever," said Jay.

"What do I have to do?" asked Emily.

"Nothing really. You'll see," said Stéphanie.

After dining on designer burgers and strong coffee the group walked a few blocks to the local shopping district. The streets buzzed with taxis and the sidewalks were full of shoppers taking advantage of the latest sales.

"In here," Stéphanie said, gesturing to head into a luxury lingerie store with large windows displaying mannequins in the latest ornate underwear and stockings with a rich red curtain behind them like from an old theatre.

"Well hello Stéphanie," said an immaculately dressed older woman with long stocking clad legs and deep red lipstick, "And who do we have here?"

"Catherine, you've met Wolf before. This is his friend Jay and this is Jay's girlfriend, Emily, our model for tonight," said Stéphanie.

Catherine shook hands with everyone and looked Emily up and down, "Yes, she is perfect. I have just the lingerie for her."

Jay and Wolf settled into a blush red settee and set about ogling Catherine's customers, picturing them in different lingerie sets on display while Stéphanie took Emily to the back room of the store.

"What am I doing?" asked Emily.

"I am organizing some publicity for the store and you are going to be the star attraction," Stéphanie said.

"Yes? Tell me more," said Emily.

"You don't have to worry about anything. I'll explain it all as we go along. First, get out of your gear and come over to the wash basin," Stéphanie said.

There was a 1950's white porcelain basin and stand at the back of the room with a small mirrored cabinet above it. Next to it was a black metal chair. With some trepidation, Emily removed her clothes, underwear, and shoes and waited for her next instruction.

"OK now stand very still," Stéphanie said, getting out a cut-throat razor and some shaving cream.

"What's that?" asked Emily looking anxious.

"Catherine's lingerie is a little high cut, so to speak, and we just need to give you a little trim before displaying you in public," Stéphanie said, stirring soap with a shaving brush and then applying the brush-up and down along Emily's pubic hair.

"Open your legs a little," Stéphanie said and when Emily had complied, brushed the shaving brush up and down between Emily's legs.

"Come on a little more. We need to get every hair," said Stéphanie, "Put one leg up on the basin."

Emily was slightly unsteady for a moment before getting her foot up onto the basin, giving Stéphanie better access between her legs.

Stéphanie applied the brush forwards and back between Emily's legs. Emily had to stifle a purr, the sensation felt so nice, the brush felt very similar to a tongue.

Once the soap lather had been applied Stéphanie then sharpened the razor on some brown leather. Stéphanie then held the blade to the light to inspect the sharpness of it. She sharpened the blade some more and then applied the blade to the inside of one of Emily's thighs and then the other.

"Leg down please," Stéphanie said then shaved down below Emily's stomach, carefully removing all of her pubic hair. Stéphanie then washed the remaining soap away and dried with a towel.

"Give me a look," Stéphanie said, peering very closely at Emily's bare private area and then pushing her nose between the folds of Emily's labia and then grabbed her buttocks and moved her head slightly back to lick up and down between Emily's legs.

"My finishing touch," Stéphanie said, "Now let's see what Catherine wants to dress you in."

Stéphanie unzipped a lingerie bag and produced an exquisite black lace lingerie set barely hanging off a black clothes hangar.

"Ah, where am I going to be modeling this?" Emily asked.

"You'll see. Now try it on. I can't wait to see how it looks on you."

Emily pulled on the black lace panties which were essentially a G string with see-through lace mesh at the front and a black ribbon that met at the top of her bottom.

"The idea is that your lover pulls the ribbon and the panties come loose," said Stéphanie.

Emily then put on the bra and found the cups of the bra were made of the same black mesh with her pink nipples clearly prominent behind the mesh. Instead of a fastener, there was a black ribbon at the back.

"I feel a little exposed," said Emily.

"It's very discrete. You are all covered and decent I assure you," said Stéphanie lying through her teeth.

"Now slip these on," said Stéphanie who opened a shoe box and produced some sky high shiny black Louboutin stilettos.

Emily almost gasped at how high the shoes were.

"I'll help you get them on," Stéphanie said, "Lift up your foot."

Emily lifted up her foot and Stéphanie held it and sucked upon Emily's toes then slipped the shoe on and strapped it up and then did the same with the other foot, Emily having to steady herself on the basin to avoid toppling over. She began to get concerned that she would soak right through those flimsy panties.

"OK let's see you walk," said Stéphanie.

Emily walked the length of the backroom like a giraffe that had just been born.

"That won't do. You need to walk like this," said Stéphanie, waking high and confidently back and forth across the room, swinging her hips.

Emily tried again, trying to emulate Stéphanie's confidence.

"Mmm. Much better. I could ravish you right here all night but you have work to do," said Stéphanie.

"You still haven't told me where you want me to model," Emily said.

"Before I do that, just one more touch," said Stéphanie wrapping a black lace mask around Emily's eyes and then applying the same red lipstick to Emily's lips as Catherine was wearing, "Catherine wants all her models to wear this lipstick. She thinks that it shows that the model is ready."

"Ready for what?" asked Emily.

"For sex of course," said Stéphanie who then playfully pinched Emily's bottom.

"Now all you need to do is go through this door over here and dance to the music. I will give you further instructions over the PA including when it's time for you to return," Stephanie said guiding Emily out through a door that led to a long corridor.

Emily opened the door at the end of the corridor and found a red curtain. She pulled along the material where the curtains joined each other aside and found herself in the shop window area.

Emily breathed in quickly and was startled, she went back behind the curtain and tried the door behind her but it had locked.

Slow tango music started on the speaker fixed to the ceiling.

Emily returned to the shop display area and looked out at the shoppers like a deer caught in the headlights.

"Relax Emily," Stéphanie's voice could be heard from the speaker.

Emily steadied herself. None of the shoppers seemed to be giving her too much attention as they rushed by.

No one can recognize you, said Emily to herself.

She closed her eyes and started to sway her hips to the music.

People from the street started to stop and watch Emily. Some of the shoppers put their hands on the glass. Some almost trip over while watching Emily and walking by. A businessman stands in front of the glass and blew a kiss to Emily.

"Blow a kiss back," Stéphanie said over the speaker.

Emily opens her eyes and blows a kiss to the crowd.

The businessman traces Emily's shape on the glass.

"Smile," Stéphanie said.

Emily smiled at the businessman who blew a kiss again and said "Hey sweetheart. Tell me that I haven't died and gone to heaven."

Emily laughed.

"Stroke the sides of your breasts," said Stéphanie.

Emily hesitated. *Could she be arrested for this?*

"Do it now," said Stéphanie.

Emily looked at the businessman and lifted her arms up and then stroked the side of each breast with the back of her hand. Emily could not help but become aroused, her nipples almost poking through the mesh of the bra.

"You're killing me," yelled out the businessman.

"Sit on the chair," Stéphanie said over the speaker.

Emily sat on the one chair in the display area. The wood was cold against her bottom.

"Now interlock your fingers between your legs and spread your legs wide," said Stéphanie.

Just hearing Stéphanie's words was scandalous to Emily. She wondered if the crowd outside could hear Stéphanie over the speaker. They seemed to be watching her very intently like she was about to reveal the mystery of the universe.

Emily interlocked her fingers and brought her hands down in front of her crotch then moved one leg out and then the other.

The crowd stirred. Some women dragged their men along the street. The businessman looked like he was going to collapse. Then there was the flash of someone taking a photograph and then another and another. A journalist was interviewing people in the street.

"Stand up and face the door and bend down and hold your ankles," said Stéphanie.

Emily felt giddy from all the attention and was now just doing everything that Stéphanie requested.

Emily stood facing the door. She felt the eyes of the crowd on her exposed buttocks. She then moved her hands down each side, past her hips and kept going down until she reached her calves.

"Just hold it there," said Stéphanie over the speaker.

Where was she watching from? wondered Emily.

"Wiggle your bottom," said Stéphanie.

Emily followed the instruction, wiggling her bottom so that her buttocks jiggled. She peered behind at the crowd that was even larger than before. Some of the crowd had their faces pressed up to the glass trying to get a better view of Emily.

"Now stand up and dance in time to the music then bow and get ready to exit," Stéphanie said.

Emily danced around the small display area, the gaze of the crowd following her from one end to the other and back.

When the music ended Emily stood where the curtains met by the doorway and bowed, the crowd fixated on Emily's cleavage.

Emily then felt a movement behind her and the curtain move slightly and then there was something pressing up against her between her legs.

"Don't move," Stéphanie said over the speaker.

Emily then felt herself being penetrated from behind. She looked behind but the curtains were still closed and Ray's penis was poking through between the two heavy red curtains.

Not knowing what to do, Emily remained bent over as Ray thrust into her, making her breasts sway forwards and backward as he pulsed into her.

Emily was afraid to look at the crowd but looked up. The crowd was enormous now and she could see the lights of a television camera crew and a cameraman filming her. Then to one side, she saw two police officers heading towards the store.

"Ray, the cops are here," hissed Emily who then quickly disappeared behind the curtain.

Emily opened the door and ran down the corridor, "I can't get arrested."

Ray followed his erection slapping him in the stomach as he ran.

Stéphanie was sitting in front of a CCTV display laughing madly.

"This way guys," said Wolf, handing them coats and holding a back door open. The four of them disappeared down an alley and into a waiting taxi.

The taxi disappeared into the stream of other taxis, leaving Catherine to explain to the police that she did not know what the model was going to do in the shop window.

The police searched the store before disbursing the crowd who were all hoping for a further glimpse of Emily.

CHAPTER 15. WHISKEY

Wolf directed the taxi to stop at his boxing gym and said to the group, "I like to come here some nights just to chill."

Emily was not sure how she felt – ashamed or exhilarated - probably a mixture of both. Jay had a protective arm around her shoulder.

Wolf paid the taxi and opened the gym, turning on a bank of lights with one switch. The group then settled in Wolf's office that overlooked the street. He produced a bottle of whiskey and poured four glasses. He put some jazz music on the stereo.

"You did good," Stéphanie said to Emily, massaging her shoulders.

Emily just raised her eyebrows.

"How did it feel being in front of all of those people," asked Jay.

"I don't know how I feel yet," said Emily.

"It was pretty hot," said Wolf.

"Where were you watching it from?" asked Emily.

"I was watching it with Steph on the CCTV," said Wolf.

"It was pretty crazy," said Jay.

"Mad," said Emily.

"It whetted my appetite," said Wolf, "Hearing Steph give you all those commands it inspired me."

"In what way?" asked Emily.

"Inspired me to control you," said Wolf.

"Only Jay gets to control me," said Emily defensively.

"Slip those panties off under that coat and toss them to me," said Wolf.

Emily looked to Jay and he nodded.

Emily reached up under the coat and pulled the panties down her legs and tossed them over to Wolf.

"I bet I could make a truckload selling these on eBay," said Wolf, "After tonight's performance these will be a collector's item. Of course, I won't tell who the famous wearer of these panties is."

Wolf dangled the panties from his finger before putting them in his pocket.

"Now Emily, tonight you are going to be our servant and wait on us hand and foot and any other part of you we care to utilize. Is that understood?" asked Wolf.

Emily bowed her head and said shyly, "Yes."

"Yes, what?" asked Wolf sternly.

"Yes, sir."

"That's better," said Wolf, "Now take that coat off and go get us all another whiskey."

"Yes, sir," said Emily who stood up and removed the long coat and stood before them in her impossibly high black stilettos, black bra and lingerie mask.

Jay thought back to when he had first met Emily and what she was like then to what she was like now. The original Emily had all but disappeared and what was before him now was some mysterious erotic princess who found herself imprisoned in the castle of a rival kingdom

Emily went to the fridge. All three of the others watched the gentle sway of her bottom as she walked.

"And put some ice in the glasses. The freezer is below the fridge," said Wolf.

Emily bent down low to get the ice and put the ice in the glasses then walked over carrying the three glasses.

Emily was about to hand out the glasses when Wolf moved his hand up between Emily's legs and started to stroke her.

"Now Emily, I demand that my waitresses be very careful in my establishment and never spill a drop of precious whiskey," said Wolf, "Is that understood?"

"Yes, sir," said Emily who hands were already starting to tremble.

"Legs further apart please Emily," said Wolf, "I need full access to your vagina at all times."

Emily wobbled slightly as she moved her legs further apart while still holding the whiskey.

Wolf removed his fingers and they glistened, "Only Jay gets to control you – that's rich. You want everyone to control you, don't you?"

Emily stood there silently, her head bowed.

"Don't you, Emily?" asked Wolf more insistently.

"Yes, sir," replied Emily.

"Emily, put the whiskey glasses down on the table, remove your bra and dip your nipples into the glasses," said Stéphanie.

Emily just stood silently.

"Emily, did you hear me?" said Stéphanie more loudly.

"Yes, ma'am," said Emily who placed the whiskey glasses on the table, untied the ribbon behind her back and released her breasts then bent down at the waist until her nipples were dipped in the whiskey.

"Hey Jay, you like a whiskey nipple don't you?" asked Wolf.

"What?" replied Jay.

"Because Emily's your girl you can have the first taste," said Wolf.

"I want first taste," said Stéphanie.

"Jay can have the right nipple and you can have the left," said Wolf.

Emily stood up and Jay came over and sucked upon her right nipple and Stéphanie came over and sucked on the left one.

"How is it?" asked Wolf.

"Delicious," said Stéphanie.

"I'm rather partial to a whiskey nipple but also like a whiskey coochie," said Wolf, "Emily, lie on the floor next to the sofa with your back on the floor and your legs resting on the sofa."

"Yes, sir," said Emily who was quickly on her back with her long legs resting on the sofa cushions.

"Now scoot towards the sofa so that you are resting on the top of your back with your legs up in the air," said Wolf.

Emily's high heeled shoes were soon pointing to the ceiling.

"Now part the lips of your coochie," said Wolf.

Emily used two fingers of her right hand to part her labia.

"Jay take a gulp of the whiskey then go down on Emily," Wolf said.

Jay picked up the glass and took a large swig. The whiskey felt like a beam of light clearing a way through him. He then cupped Emily's buttocks with both hands and licked in a long line between Emily's legs with just the right amount of pressure to make Emily squirm with pleasure. After licking up and down between Emily's legs he then found Emily's bud with his tongue and lightly massaged it, his mouth deliciously warm with the whiskey.

"My turn now brother," said Wolf who came over and inspected Emily who was still holding the lips of her sex open with two fingers.

Wolf cupped each of Emily's breasts and rubbed her nipples between his fingers and then placed one finger deep into her and lightly caressed her G spot.

"Nothing like a whiskey coochie," said Wolf.

"Emily, bend over the glass of whiskey over there and see if you can drink it without holding the glass. Just use your tongue," said Stéphanie.

Emily bent over the glass of whiskey on the table, was a little unsteady on her high heels for a moment then stuck her tongue into the whiskey glass and lapped at it like a cat.

"Good kitty," said Stéphanie stroking Emily's bottom like patting a cat.

"I think we should reward her with a whiskey nipple," said Wolf, "Emily go sit on the couch with your legs wide apart."

Emily followed Wolf's instruction, perched upon the black leather couch with her legs splayed.

Wolf walked over and grabbed the bottle of whiskey and poured it over Emily's breasts and down her body and between her legs, warming her labia.

"Now treat yourself to two whiskey nipples," said Wolf.

Emily looked confused.

Stéphanie pointed to her own breasts and lent down and pretended to lick one.

Emily then held one breast up to her mouth and tried to lick it. Her tongue stretched trying to reach the nipple and she held her breast as high as she could but could not quite reach it with her mouth. She tried the other breast but had the same problem.

"Well if Emily cannot enjoy a whiskey nipple then maybe she can have a taste of whiskey coochie," said Wolf, "Steph, would you oblige."

Stéphanie sat down next to Emily and pulled down her short glittery skirt and panties and spread her legs as wide as Emily's legs were spread.

"What a beautiful sight," said Wolf, "Two gorgeous, adventuress women wild for the night."

Jay nodded while sipping on his whiskey.

"Would you wet the whistle so to speak?" said Wolf.

Jay put two fingers into the glass and fished out a cube of ice and rubbed the whiskey and ice over Stéphanie's labia and pushed the ice cube within the lips then it slipped out again. He did this a few times.

"That's so cold," said Stéphanie, "Emily, you come warm me up."

Emily then got down on the floor between Emily's legs and licked Emily's labia up and down.

"Try long licks like a cat," said Wolf.

Emily slowed down her licking up and down along Emily's labia, emulating a cat licking fur.

"Good kitty," said Stéphanie, stroking Emily's head which was buried between her legs.

"Legs apart, Emily," said Jay from behind.

Emily moved her knees apart as she continued to lick up and down between Stéphanie's legs.

Jay lay on the ground and leaned up between Emily's legs, performing cunnilingus on Emily while Emily did the same on Stéphanie.

Wolf then approached the group. He had already removed his trousers but not his shirt. Stéphanie raised her eyebrows at the size of his erection and soon had her lips wrapped around it as it slid in and out of her mouth.

"Let's have a race as to who can come first. But no cheating. Ladies, I mean you," said Wolf, "As men, it's pretty apparent if we are coming or not. With you ladies, it is a bit of a mystery. Well to me anyway."

All of the others had their mouth too full to express an opinion.

Jay wanted Emily to come first and used his fingers and tongue to stimulate her, fingering, licking and sucking, and she squirmed above him.

Stéphanie tongue was licking up and down Wolf's shaft with abandon while she cupped his balls in her hand and squeezed the head of his cock with her other hand.

Emily was now delicately sucking on Stéphanie's clit and Stéphanie seemed very close to orgasm.

Wolf then smacked his hand down onto Emily's buttocks, leaving a red handprint upon her. For some reason, the smack and the earnest licking and sucking by Jay send her over the ledge and she was freefalling into pleasure.

"We have a winner," said Wolf.

CHAPTER 16. EUPHORIA

The next morning Jay woke up and looked over at Emily sleeping next to him in his sun-filled bedroom. *She is so beautiful*, thought Jay.

"What?" asked Emily, waking up and seeing Jay looking at her.

"Just thinking about how you may serve me today," said Jay.

"And what did you decide?" asked Emily.

"First go to the shower and bring yourself to the verge of orgasm in the shower," said Jay, "And then await my instructions."

Emily nodded and walked naked to Jay's bathroom. Since Stéphanie had shaved all the pubic hair from Emily she looked even more naked than before.

The shower was hot and refreshing for Emily and she lathered the soap on.

Jay walked over and opened the glass shower screen door and pulled up a chair.

"Proceed, Emily," he said.

Emily soaped her breasts, working the soap into a thick layer that covered them and used her fingers to pinch and pull upon her nipples.

"Good girl," said Jay.

Emily then rubbed the soap on her stomach, keeping her gaze upon Jay. She then slipped the soap between her legs, working it into a lather and then getting the shower nozzle and washing the soap away but keeping the shower stream between her legs to stimulate her clit. Emily momentarily closed her eyes, enjoying the moment.

"Did I tell you not to come?" Jay said in a somewhat angry tone.

"I wasn't coming, Jay," said Emily meekly.

"Bend over please," said Jay.

Emily presented her wet bottom to Jay through the shower stall.

Jay spanked her buttocks once with one hand.

"What do you say, Emily?"

"Thank you," Emily said, moving back into the shower stall.

"Thank you what?" asked Jay.

"Thank you, sir," said Emily.

"Much better," said Jay.

"Should I continue, sir?" Emily said, not sure what to do next.

"Don't presume to tell me what you should do. Await your instructions, Emily," said Jay sternly.

Emily loved how Jay was being so dominant and longed to have him inside her.

"Now imagine your thumb is my penis. Show me how you would like to suck it," said Jay.

The shower water streamed over Emily, steaming up the bathroom while Emily performed fellatio on her thumb, maintaining eye contact with Jay the whole time.

"Now imagine I am penetrating you from behind. Bounce upon your thumb like it is my cock and show me how much you enjoy it," said Jay.

Emily twisted her arm around and penetrated herself with her thumb and moved back and forward with a look of ecstasy upon her face.

"I told you not to come!" said Jay in mock indignation

"I was just acting," said Emily.

"So you just pretend to come when I penetrate you?" said Jay, playfully.

"No, sir," said Emily.

"Bend over," said Jay.

Emily again presented her bottom to Jay through the shower stall and he smacked her quickly upon the buttocks, causing a warm rush of endorphins to her head. She wanted to let go of everything and surrender everything to her lover.

"Thank you, sir," said Emily.

"My pleasure," said Jay contentedly, "OK now dry yourself and then go bend over the dining table."

Jay watched as Emily dried herself and then padded over to the dining table in the living area and lay down upon it with her bottom facing Jay.

"Move your head up a little," said Jay as he wrapped a blindfold around Emily's eyes.

Jay then tested just how aroused Emily was by rubbing his finger along her labia and was pleased with the level of wetness. He loved how much Emily was into this and how aroused she was. It was such a turn on for him.

"OK Emily, now stand up and stretch your arms up to the ceiling," Jay said.

Emily immediately stood up and reached her hands up high. Jay loved watching a woman stretch. It was one of the perks of being a personal trainer.

"Higher," said Jay.

"Yes, sir," said Emily standing on the tips of her toes.

"Now hold that. Let me inspect you," said Jay.

Jay stepped forward and held both of Emily's breasts as she remained on the tips of her toes. He massaged them and then rubbed her nipples between his fingers and felt them stiffen then slightly pulled them a couple of times.

"Very nice," said Jay, "OK Emily now keep your hands up in the air and I want you to hump the table."

Emily had a quizzical look on her face. She put one hand down to feel where the table was.

"Did I tell you to put your hand down?" Jay said sternly.

"No, sir," said Emily.

"Bend over," said Jay.

Emily bent over the table again and her bottom was met with a quick spank.

"Now, let's try again, shall we?" Jay said, admiring the red handprint on Emily's pale skin.

Emily raised her hands again up high and positioned herself at the corner of the table and moved forward and back on the edge of the table, grinding her clit against it and moaning quietly.

Jay sat and watched Emily humping the table for a couple of minutes. Emily liked putting on a show for Jay and putting herself in his hands and just focusing on what she was feeling and experiencing.

"OK, now play with your breasts as you do that. Twist and pull your nipples," said Jay.

Emily road the table whilst pulling upon her breasts, her nipples pointing upwards to the ceiling.

"Now let's see how wet you are. Bend over the table again with your legs far apart," said Jay.

Emily did as requested. Jay's fingers slipped easily in and out of Emily who was positively dripping with arousal.

"Good girl," said Jay and Emily felt satisfied in pleasing Jay and accomplishing the tasks correctly and earning praise. It made her feel wanted.

Jay loved having Emily trust him so completely and happily surrendering her will to his desires. It was deeply satisfying and made him both feel powerful and humbled. Jay wanted to honor that trust.

Jay unzipped and eased his erection into Emily smoothly until she was filled to the brim with him. Jay thrust deeply in and out of Emily, massaging her buttocks with his hands.

Jay then withdrew and said, "Turn around Emily and spread your legs."

"Yes, sir," said Emily.

Emily turned around and rested her bottom against the edge of the table and spread her legs wide.

Jay immediately entered her and felt the hard nipples of her breasts rub against his chest and he reached down and used his hand to finger Emily's clit while he thrust into her.

Emily had her eyes closed.

"Open your eyes," said Jay.

Emily said breathlessly, "Yes, oh, sir."

"Did I say you could come yet?"

"No, oh, sir."

Jay directed his thrusting to Emily's G spot, making her breath faster and more intensely while still stimulating her clit with his fingers, driving her almost insane with erotic pressure, like she was on the edge of a cliff and was about to hang glide off it. Emily summonsed every cell in her being to stay on that cliff until Jay told her she was allowed to orgasm.

"Oh, please sir, let me come," said Emily.

"Tell me how much you want it," said Jay, who was also breathless and almost at the point of orgasm.

"I want it more than anything," said Emily.

"What do you want?" asked Jay.

"I want to feel you release inside me while I come," said Emily panting.

"OK, Emily suck on my nipples while I do you," said Jay.

Emily leaned forward and sucked on one nipple while stroking the other nipple with her hand and then sucking the other while using her hand on the other.

Jay closed his eyes. *This is too much*, thought Jay.

"Now kiss me," said Jay and they kissed each other deeply.

Emily was moaning with pleasure.

"Now you may come," said Jay pulsing into Emily as her body trembled with euphoria.

CHAPTER 17. FIRE

"Where have you been? I've been getting worried about you," said Mia giving Emily a hug in greeting at their favorite Starbucks.

"Oh you know," said Emily.

"You mean Jay is monopolizing you," laughed Mia.

Emily leaned in and said quietly, "Mia, I'm worried I am becoming a sex addict."

Mia laughed.

"I mean I think about it all the time," said Emily looking very concerned.

"Yeah, like most of the population. That's only natural," said Mia.

"I feel like now I have turned the sex button on I cannot turn it off," said Emily.

"Why would you want to turn it off? You waited too long to turn it on in the first place if you ask me," said Mia, her hand stroking Emily's leg under the table.

Emily raised her eyebrows, "It feels like I am on fire and nothing can put it out."

"Don't put it out. Stoke it," said Mia, her fingers creeping up Emily's thigh.

"And Jay – wow. Just thinking about him makes me – you know," said Emily.

Mia sipped on her coffee while simultaneously brushing her fingers up and down the front of Emily's panties.

"You are wet," Mia whispered.

Mia continued to probe. She seemed to Emily to know exactly where to touch, how hard to press and the right rhythm to keep. Emily found it hard to keep her coffee cup steady.

Emily looked around the café at the other customers. They were all either checking their phones or deep in conversation. There was one man reading the newspaper. He flipped over the page and there was a photograph of Emily in the storefront of Catherine's lingerie store. The article was titled "Only in New York". Catherine's store soon became the most infamous and popular lingerie store in New York.

Meeting Jay had ignited a spark in Emily. One that she felt would never be extinguished.

Thanks for reading!
Please add a short review on the web store where you purchased this book and let us know what you thought!

For information on hot new releases and a free erotica ebook subscribe to

Don't miss out!

Visit the website below and you can sign up to receive emails whenever Nicolas Blanc publishes a new book. There's no charge and no obligation.

https://books2read.com/r/B-A-IHVC-YBOX

BOOKS2READ

Connecting independent readers to independent writers.